For Mom and Frank, with love
—K. D.

For Mom, Dad, and Brian
—S. C.

ATHENEUM BOOKS FOR YOUNG READERS
An imprint of Simon & Schuster Children's Publishing Division
1230 Avenue of the Americas
New York, New York 10020
Text copyright © 2011 by Kelly DiPucchio
Illustrations copyright © 2011 by Scott Campbell
ATHENEUM BOOKS FOR YOUNG READERS is a registered trademark of Simon & Schuster, Inc.
For information about special discounts for bulk purchases, please contact Simon &
Schuster Special Sales at 1-866-506-1949 or business@simonandschuster.com.
The Simon & Schuster Speakers Bureau can bring authors to your live event. For more
information or to book an event, contact the Simon & Schuster Speakers Bureau at
1-866-248-3049 or visit our website at www.simonspeakers.com.
Book design by Sonia Chaghatzbanian
The text for this book is set in Barbera.
The illustrations for this book are rendered in watercolor.
Manufactured in China
0414 SCP

8 10 9 7
Library of Congress Cataloging-in-Publication Data
DiPucchio, Kelly S.
Zombie in love / Kelly DiPucchio ; illustrated by Scott Campbell. — 1st ed.
p. cm.
Summary: When all his efforts to find a sweetheart fail, Mortimer the zombie
decides to place an ad in the newspaper.
ISBN 978-1-4424-0270-6 (hardcover)
[1. Zombies—Fiction. 2. Humorous stories.] I. Campbell, Scott, ill. II. Title.
PZ7.D6219Zm 2010
[E]—dc22   2009025640

Zombie in Love

Kelly DiPucchio

pictures by
Scott Campbell

Atheneum Books for Young Readers
New York London Toronto Sydney

Mortimer was lonely.

Cupid's Ball was just a few weeks away and he didn't have a sweetheart. Oh, he tried, but somehow the ladies didn't appreciate Mortimer's affections.

He gave the girl at the bus stop
a fancy box of chocolates.

He gave the mail carrier a shiny, red heart.

And he gave the waitress at the diner a stunning diamond ring.

Poor Mortimer.

ead books and followed
the advice.

He took his dog for a walk
in the park.

He worked out at the gym.

He even took ballroom dancing lessons.

But nothing he did seemed to impress the girls.

Then Mortimer got an idea.

He placed an ad in the newspaper.

TALL, DEAD, & HANDSOME

If you like taking walks in the
  graveyard
and falling down in the rain.
If you're not into cooking,
if you have half a brain.
If you like waking up at midnight,
horror films, and voodoo,
then I'm the guy who you've
  looked for
and I'm dying to meet you!

Saturday, Cupid's Ball,
Punch Bowl, 7:00 p.m.

Mortimer was sure this was the answer!

On Saturday he shopped
for a new suit.

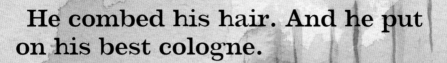

He combed his hair. And he put on his best cologne.

Cupid's Ball was hopping! Couples were dancing and laughing and, well ... having a ball.

And waited.

And waited.

Each time a girl approached
the table, Mortimer would smile.

Like this:

And each time the girl would
shriek and run away.

He tried breath mints.

He tried handing out roses.

He tried being funny.

Nothing worked.

As the night wore on,
the room began to empty.

The punch bowl did not.

Suddenly it became clear to Mortimer that *nobody* was dying to meet him.

He began to shuffle toward the exit when he heard a loud thud. The thud was followed by an even louder crash.

Mortimer turned around.
There on the floor was a girl.

Her name was Mildred and she
was drop-dead gorgeous.

She smiled.

Like this:

Mildred stood up and shook the pineapple rings from her hair.

"Am I too late?" she asked.

The clock struck midnight.

"You're right on time," said Mortimer.

Mortimer and Mildred danced.

And held hands.

And dined
by the moonlight.

It was love at first bite.